WORKBOOK FOR

THE GRAPHIC NOVEL

HEINLE
CENGAGE Learning™

Australia • Brazil • Japan • Korea • Mexico • Singapore • Spain • United Kingdom • United States

HEINLE
CENGAGE Learning™

Workbook for The Tempest:
The Graphic Novel

Publisher: Sherrise Roehr
Editor in Chief: Clive Bryant
Associate Development Editor: Cécile Engeln
Director of U.S. Marketing: Jim McDonough
Assistant Marketing Manager: Jide Iruka
Director of Content Production: Michael Burggren
Associate Content Project Manager:
 Mark Rzeszutek
Print Buyer: Sue Spencer
Character Designs and Original Artwork:
 Jon Haward
Inking: Gary Erskine
Coloring and Lettering: Nigel Dobbyn
Color/Text Design & Layout: Jo Wheeler
 and Carl Andrews
Compositor: MPS Limited, a Macmillan Company

For product information and technology assistance, contact us at
Cengage Learning Customer & Sales support, 1-800-354-9706

For permission to use material from this text or product,
submit all requests online at **www.cengage.com/permissions**
Further permissions questions can be e-mailed to
permissionrequest@cengage.com

ISBN 13: 978-1-111-22006-8

ISBN 10: 1-111-22006-9

Heinle
20 Channel Center Street
Boston, MA 02210
USA

Cengage Learning is a leading provider of customised learning solutions with office locations around the globe, including Singapore, the United Kingdom, Australia, Mexico, Brazil and Japan. Locate our local office at:
international.cengage.com/region

Cengage Learning products are represented in Canada by Nelson Education, Ltd.

Visit Heinle online at **elt.heinle.com**

Visit our corporate website at **www.cengage.com**

Printed in the United States of America
5 6 7 8 9 10 11 24 23 22 21 20

CONTENTS

Name: _____

A. Choose the best answer to each question by circling the letter of the correct answer.

1. William Shakespeare was born in _____.
   a. London   **b.** Gloucester   **c.** Stratford-upon-Avon   **d.** Salisbury

2. His father was _____.
   a. a wealthy nobleman   **b.** a farmer   **c.** very poor   **d.** a tradesman

3. Shakespeare's wife's name was _____.
   a. Mary   **b.** Elizabeth   **c.** Anne   **d.** Helen

4. Shakespeare wrote a total of _____ plays.
   a. 24   **b.** 38   **c.** 42   **d.** 16

5. He had three children, _____.
   a. two boys and a girl   **b.** all girls   **c.** all boys   **d.** two girls and a boy

6. Shakespeare lived in Elizabethan England. This means he lived during a time _____.
   a. when Elizabeth was a popular name
   b. when Elizabeth I was Queen
   c. in the time of Queen Elizabeth II
   d. in an area of Britain called Elizabeth

Now read about Shakespeare on p. 138–139 of *The Tempest: The Graphic Novel* and find out if you were right.

B. Complete the timeline of Shakespeare's life.

Shakespeare Timeline

Approximate Date	What Happened?
1564	
1582	He married . . .
1583–1585	
1587	
1590–1613	
1593	
1616	
1670	

C. Circle the titles of the plays that were written by Shakespeare.

Romeo and Juliet   *The Merchant of Venice*   *The White Devil*   *King Lear*
Macbeth   *Tamburlaine*   *Othello*   *A Midsummer Night's Dream*

D. Can you name any other Shakespeare plays? Make a list.

Name: _____

A. Read "The History of the Tempest" on pp. 140–141. Then circle the answer that best completes each statement below.

    1. *The Tempest* is believed to be the _____ play that Shakespeare wrote alone.

        a. only   **b.** first   **c.** second   **d.** last

    2. *The Tempest* is Shakespeare's only play that _____.

        a. features Italian characters

        b. includes magic

        c. begins with a shipwreck

        d. has no earlier source for its story

    3. The "Lost Colony" was in _____.

        a. North America   **b.** Bermuda   **c.** Africa   **d.** Asia

    4. The character of Caliban was probably inspired by _____.

        a. Columbus

        b. strange stories that travelers brought back about native peoples

        c. King James I

        d. the survivors in "A Discovery of the Bermudas, other wise called the Ile of Divels"

    5. Which of the following people is NOT thought to be an inspiration for the character of Prospero?

        a. William Shakespeare   **b.** King James I   **c.** Sir Walter Raleigh   **d.** Dr. John Dee

B. Read "Shakespeare's Globe Theatre" on pp. 142–143. Match the dates with the events.

    1. _____ 1576   **a.** The Second Globe Theatre is built.

    2. _____ 1598   **b.** The Theatre is built.

    3. _____ 1613   **c.** The New Globe Theatre officially opens.

    4. _____ 1614   **d.** The Puritans shut down all theaters, and performances stop.

    5. _____ 1642   **e.** The Theatre is taken apart and rebuilt as the Globe Theatre on the other side of the Thames River.

    6. _____ 1997   **f.** The Globe Theatre burns down.

C. How was the Blackfriars Theatre different from the Globe Theatre? What did they have in common? Fill in the Venn diagram.

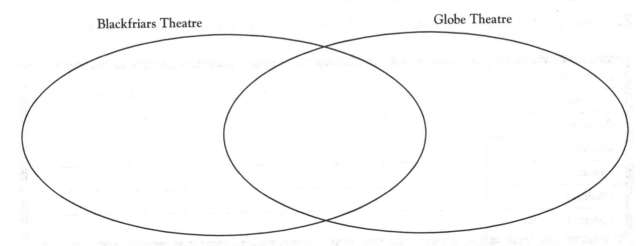

Blackfriars Theatre   Globe Theatre

Name: _____

Before You Read
Worksheet 3 – Prepare to Discuss the Play

A. Shakespeare wrote three different kinds of plays: comedies, tragedies, and histories. Match the definitions below with the kind of play by writing the letter of the correct definition.

1. _____ comedy
2. _____ tragedy
3. _____ history

a. a serious play with a sad ending
b. a play based on the life of an English king
c. a lighthearted play with a happy ending

B. A **play** is organized into acts and scenes. An **act** is one of the main parts into which a play is divided; it can contain several scenes. A **scene** is a series of events that occur in the same place.

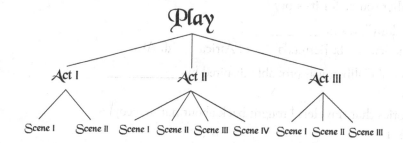

Look at the Contents for *The Tempest* on p. 3. How many acts does *The Tempest* have?

_____

C. Match the parts of a play with their definitions.

1. _____ plot
2. _____ prologue
3. _____ dialogue
4. _____ climax
5. _____ epilogue
6. _____ setting

a. the words that the characters say
b. the story of a play
c. the turning point or most exciting part of a play
d. where a play takes place
e. a speech that introduces a play
f. concluding speech at the end of a play

D. Now match the types of characters with their descriptions.

1. _____ character
2. _____ protagonist
3. _____ villain

a. the most important person in a play
b. the evil person in a play
c. a person in a play

E. As you read *The Tempest*, complete the chart below with examples of each term from the play.

protagonist	Prospero
prologue	
dialogue	
setting	
climax	
villain(s)	
epilogue	

Name: _____

Worksheet 4 – Meet the Characters

A. Cut out the pictures of the characters. Then glue or tape them in the correct spaces below.

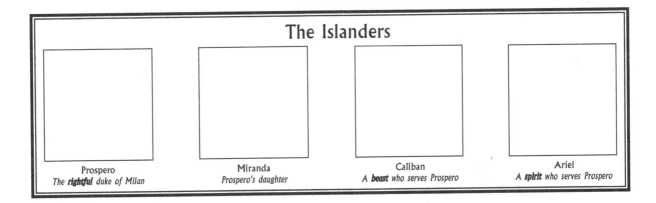

The Islanders

Prospero	Miranda	Caliban	Ariel
The rightful duke of Milan	*Prospero's daughter*	*A beast who serves Prospero*	*A spirit who serves Prospero*

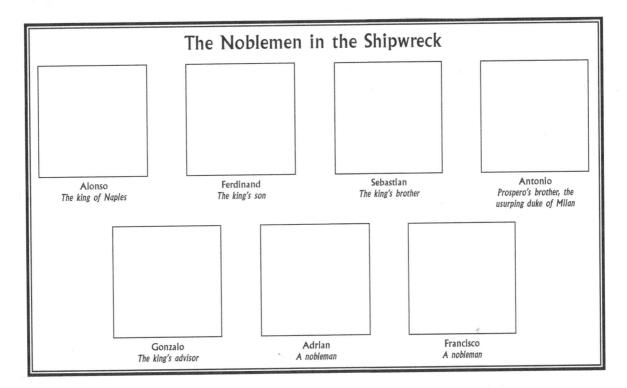

The Noblemen in the Shipwreck

Alonso	Ferdinand	Sebastian	Antonio
The king of Naples	*The king's son*	*The king's brother*	*Prospero's brother, the usurping duke of Milan*

Gonzalo	Adrian	Francisco
The king's advisor	*A nobleman*	*A nobleman*

Servants in the Shipwreck

Stephano	Trinculo
A drunken butler	*A jester*

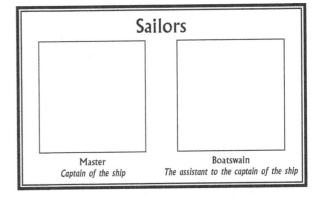

Sailors

Master	Boatswain
Captain of the ship	*The assistant to the captain of the ship*

Before You Read
Worksheet 1 – Meet the Characters

A. Cut out the pictures of the characters. Then glue or tape them onto the spaces below.

The Islanders

Ariel

Caliban
A half-monster, Prospero

Miranda
Prospero's daughter

Prospero
The rightful duke of Milan

The Noblemen in the Shipwreck

Antonio
Prospero's brother, the reigning duke of Milan

Sebastian
The king's brother

Ferdinand
The prince

Alonso
The king of Naples

Francisco
A nobleman

Adrian
A nobleman

Gonzalo
The king's advisor

Sailors

Boatswain
The officer in command of the ship

Master
Captain of the ship

Servants in the Shipwreck

Trinculo
A jester

Stephano
A drunken butler

Cut out the pictures of the characters. Glue or tape them in the correct places on Worksheet 4.

Name: _____

A. Complete the story summary below using the words from the word bank.

servants	island	wedding	son
advisor	magician	Africa	traveling
terrible	usurped	Tunis	ship
spirit	beautiful	storm	ugly
Naples	brother	Mediterranean	Milan

The Tempest

This story takes place on a strange 1. _____ in the 2. _____ Sea. A man named Prospero lives there with his 3. _____ daughter, Miranda. He also has two 4. _____: an 5. _____ creature named Caliban, and a cheerful 6. _____ named Ariel.

Prospero is now a 7. _____. Before he came to the island, he was the duke of 8. _____. The current duke is Prospero's brother, Antonio. Antonio 9. _____ the title of duke from Prospero many years before.

At the beginning of the story, Antonio is on a 10. _____ sailing from North 11. _____. He is 12. _____ with Alonso, the king of 13. _____, Alonso's 14. _____, Ferdinand, and Alonso's 15. _____, Sebastian. They are joined by the king's 16. _____, Gonzalo, who was once a friend of Prospero's. The men on the ship are returning from the 17. _____ of Alonso's daughter to the king of 18. _____. However, on the way back home, they encounter a 19. _____ 20. _____ that shipwrecks them on Prospero's island!

B. Answer the questions.

1. Do you think it is a coincidence that the ship carrying Prospero's brother is shipwrecked on the island where Prospero is living? Explain.

_____

_____

2. Do you think anyone is killed in the shipwreck? Explain.

_____

_____

3. How do you think Prospero feels about his brother? What do you think will happen if they meet on the island?

_____

_____

_____

While You Read

Worksheet 6 – Act I, Scene I

A. Listen to the audio for Act I, Scene I as you follow along on pp. 8–13. Then read the statements below and decide if they are true or false. Circle your answers. If the statement is false, make it true and write it on the lines.

1. Prospero is creating the storm using magic.   True   False
_____

2. The boatswain wants the king and his men to help the sailors.   True   False
_____

3. Gonzalo is afraid because he thinks the boatswain doesn't know what he's doing.   True   False
_____

4. Gonzalo wants to fight with the boatswain.   True   False
_____

5. The ship starts breaking apart.   True   False
_____

6. The men think they are going to die.   True   False
_____

B. Circle the correct definition for each word in **bold**.
1. Captain: "Make those sailors work harder or we'll **sink**!"
    a. to disappear below the surface of a mass of water
    b. to die from being underwater and not being able to breathe
    c. a large fixed container that supplies water
2. Gonzalo: "That boatswain makes me feel safe. He won't **drown**."
    a. to drink too much alcohol
    b. to die from being underwater and not being able to breathe
    c. to crash a ship
3. Boatswain: "Bring down that top **sail**!"
    a. to move across the water using the wind as power
    b. the top part of a ship that forms a floor in the open air which you can walk on
    c. a piece of material attached to the mast of a ship
4. Sebastian: "Be quiet, you **loudmouth**!"
    a. a person who speaks loudly and offensively
    b. a large creature that looks very ugly and frightening
    c. the noise made by a group of people clapping their hands
5. Boatswain: "You **sail** the ship, then!"
    a. to make something disappear below the surface of a mass of water
    b. a piece of material attached to the mast of a ship
    c. to move a boat across the water
6. Antonio: "We're being drowned by a bunch of **drunks**!"
    a. large and dangerous animals
    b. people who have had a lot of alcohol
    c. people who speak loudly and offensively

While You Read

Worksheet 7 – Act I, Scene II

CD 1
Track 3

A. Listen to the audio as you read Act I, Scene II, pp. 14–24. Circle the correct word or phrase to complete each statement.

1. Miranda was **a baby/three years old** when she and her father left Italy.

2. Miranda is now **twelve/fifteen** years old.

3. Prospero let Antonio rule in his place while he **traveled/studied**.

4. Then, Antonio worked with **Sebastian/Alonso** to get rid of Prospero.

5. **Miranda's mother/Gonzalo** helped Prospero and Miranda escape safely.

CD 1
Track 3

B. Continue reading Act I, Scene II, on pp. 25–37. Then compare Ariel and Caliban in the chart.

	Ariel	**Caliban**
Physical appearance	small, light, has wings . . .	
Personality/abilities		
How he became Prospero's servant		
Attitude about being Prospero's servant		

C. Circle the vocabulary word that doesn't fit with the others.

1. hell   decent   devil   evil
2. goddess   maiden   monster   nymph
3. spy   enemy   traitor   noble
4. freedom   servant   butler   slave

While You Read
Worksheet 7 – Act I, Scene II (continued)

CD 1
Track 3

D. Listen to the audio as you read Act I, Scene II, pp. 38–44. Answer the questions.

1. Why does Ferdinand go to Prospero's house?

_____

_____

2. Why does Prospero want Ferdinand to come to him?

_____

_____

3. What does Miranda think of Ferdinand when she first sees him?

_____

_____

4. What does Ferdinand think of Miranda when he first sees her?

_____

_____

5. Why does Prospero accuse Ferdinand of being a spy and a traitor?

_____

_____

E. Imagine your classroom is the set of a talk show called "Good Morning, Naples!" On today's show, the guests are Caliban and Prospero. Caliban will argue that Prospero treats him unfairly, while Prospero will argue that his treatment is justified. Surprise guests will include Miranda (in favor of Prospero) and Ariel (in favor of Caliban). Audience members will also be able to give their opinions.

You will play one of the following roles: the host, Caliban, Prospero, Miranda, Ariel, or an audience member. Try to imagine what your character would think and feel about the topic. Then, try to imagine what your opponents' arguments will be. Write your arguments and counterarguments below.

My role: _____ I support (circle one): Caliban   Prospero

My arguments: _____

_____

_____

_____

Opponents' possible arguments: _____

_____

_____

_____

My counterarguments: _____

_____

_____

_____

_____

Name: _____

CD 1
Track 4

A. Listen to Act II, Scene I, and read along on pp. 45–64. Then complete the sentences with words from the word bank.

gloomy	barren	drawn	heir
loss	swamp	throne	miracle

1. A person's _____ has a right to inherit that person's money, property, or title.
2. A _____ is a decorative chair used by a king, queen, or emperor.
3. Land that has soil so poor that plants cannot grow in it is _____.
4. An area of very wet land with wild plants growing in it is a _____.
5. A _____ is a very surprising and fortunate event.
6. People who are unhappy and have no hope are _____.
7. You experience a _____ if you no longer have something or have less of it.
8. A sword that is removed from its sheath is _____.

B. Decide if the statements about Act II, Scene I are true or false. Circle your answer.

1. Alonso is pleased with Gonzalo's efforts to comfort him.   True   False
2. Antonio and Sebastian try to comfort Alonso.   True   False
3. Adrian thinks that the island is a nice place.   True   False
4. Dido is Alonso's daughter.   True   False
5. Ancient Carthage is now Tunis.   True   False
6. Francisco tries to convince Alonso that Ferdinand is dead.   True   False

C. Answer the questions.

1. Describe Antonio and Sebastian. How do they treat the people with them? Explain your answers.

_____

_____

_____

_____

_____

2. What does Antonio convince Sebastian to do? Why?

_____

_____

_____

_____

_____

3. Does their plan succeed? Why or why not? How do they cover up their plan?

_____

_____

_____

_____

_____

Name: _____

While You Read
Worksheet 9 – Act II, Scene II

A. Listen to Act II, Scene II, as you follow along on pp. 65–74. Circle the name of the character who said each quote.

1. "They'd pay money to see this thing in England."   Caliban   Stephano   Trinculo
2. "We loved all the girls, except Kate, she was full of insults and hate."   Caliban   Stephano   Trinculo
3. "I'm from the moon. I'm the man on the moon."   Caliban   Stephano   Trinculo
4. "He's a worthless, dirty monster!"   Caliban   Stephano   Trinculo
5. "I'll show you where to find fresh water and food."   Caliban   Stephano   Trinculo
6. "I'll never catch another fish, or scrape a plate or wash a dish."   Caliban   Stephano   Trinculo

B. Read the summary of Act II, Scene II. Fill in the blanks with words from the word bank.

freedom	tame	heaven	torture	swear
shelter	devil	monster	shore	butler

At the beginning of the scene, Caliban is standing on the 1. _____. He is angry because Prospero's spirits 2. _____ him. He sees Trinculo coming, so he hides. Trinculo sees a storm coming and takes 3. _____ with Caliban.

Soon, Stephano, the 4. _____, arrives. He is drinking wine and singing a song. Then, there is some confusion! Stephano thinks Caliban is a 5. _____. He wants to 6. _____ Caliban and sell him.

When Stephano hears Trinculo speak, he thinks Caliban has two mouths. Trinculo thinks that the person speaking must be a 7. _____, because he thinks that Stephano drowned. Meanwhile, Caliban thinks that Stephano and Trinculo are both spirits. After Caliban tastes Stephano's wine, he changes his mind. Caliban thinks that Stephano must be a god from 8. _____.

Stephano makes Caliban 9. _____ that Caliban will be his servant. Caliban is happy now, because he believes he has found 10. _____ from Prospero.

C. Answer the questions.
1. What does Trinculo think when he first sees Caliban?

_____

_____

2. How did Stephano survive the shipwreck?

_____

_____

3. At the end of the scene, Trinculo says that Caliban is pathetic. What does he mean by this? How does Trinculo treat Caliban?

_____

_____

_____

_____

While You Read

Worksheet 10 – Act III, Scene I

CD 1
Track 6

A. Read Act III, Scene I, pp. 75–79, and listen to the audio. Write the definition of each vocabulary word. Then, explain how each word is used in the story.

1. admire: _____

_____

2. heaven: _____

_____

3. bless: _____

_____

B. Decide whether the statements are true or false. Correct the false statements and write them on the lines.

1. The setting of Act III, Scene I, is outside Caliban's cave.   True   False

_____

2. Ferdinand is looking for food for Prospero.   True   False

_____

3. Ferdinand thinks that Prospero is kind.   True   False

_____

4. Prospero told Miranda not to tell Ferdinand her name.   True   False

_____

5. Prospero is busy studying and doesn't see what's happening between Ferdinand
   and Miranda.   True   False

_____

6. Prospero is angry that Miranda disobeyed him.   True   False

_____

C. Fill in the chart with examples of what Miranda and Ferdinand say to express their love for each other.

Expressions of Love

Ferdinand	Miranda
"She's ten times more beautiful than her father is mean." (p. 75)	

Name: _____

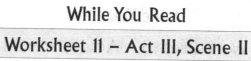
A. Read and listen to Act III, Scene II, pp. 80–85. Then fill in the blanks with words from the word bank.

CD 1
Track 7

lord	kneel	trance	governors
servant	trick	revenge	challenges

Caliban's Plans

Caliban is angry and wants 1. _____ on Prospero. He believes that Prospero used his magic to 2. _____ him. Prospero took the island from Caliban and made Caliban his 3. _____. Now, Caliban wants Stephano to be his master instead. Caliban calls Stephano "4. _____." Stephano asks Caliban to 5. _____ in front of him to show respect. Caliban 6. _____ Stephano to find Prospero and kill him. Then, Stephano can be king of the island and make Caliban and Trinculo 7. _____.

While Caliban, Stephano, and Trinculo walk towards Prospero's house, they hear strange music. Stephano and Trinculo are afraid, but Caliban tells them not to worry. He says the music puts him in a 8. _____ sometimes and gives him beautiful dreams.

B. Answer the questions.

1. Why do Trinculo and Stephano fight at the beginning of the scene?

   _____

   _____

   _____

2. Describe the plan for revenge that Caliban tells Stephano.
   a. First, Stephano should . . .

   _____

   _____

   b. Then, he should . . .

   _____

   _____

   c. After that, he can . . .

   _____

   _____

3. Why do you think Caliban asks Stephano to do this instead of doing it himself?

   _____

   _____

   _____

4. Do you think Caliban's plan will succeed? What do you think will happen?

   _____

   _____

Name: _____

CD 1
Track 8

A. Read Act III, Scene III, pp. 86–94, and listen to the audio. Complete the sentences with the missing information from the story.

1. The men are walking, but _____ says that he is tired and needs to rest.
2. Alonso has lost hope and decides to stop looking for _____.
3. Meanwhile, Antonio and Sebastian decide to _____.
4. Then, Alonso and Gonzalo hear some _____.
5. Suddenly, a _____ appears in front of them. It has a lot of _____ on it.
6. _____ picks up a fruit, but he stops in fear before he can eat it.
7. A huge, scary _____ appears and tells Alonso, Antonio, and Sebastian that they are evil men because _____.
8. Prospero, who is watching, feels happy because _____.

B. Explain the meaning of each underlined vocabulary word from Act III, Scene III.

1. "They're all <u>exhausted</u> from traveling."
   _____
   _____

2. "These strange <u>natives</u> seem so kind."
   _____
   _____

3. "Travelers often bring back stories of strange things and strange <u>creatures</u>."
   _____
   _____

4. "<u>Foolish</u> men! Your swords won't work against us!"
   _____
   _____

5. "You must be <u>sincerely</u> sorry for what you have done and promise to live good lives from now on."
   _____
   _____

6. "All three of them have gone crazy. Their <u>guilt</u> is affecting them."
   _____
   _____

C. Answer the questions.

1. According to the fiery spirit, what will happen if the men are not sincerely sorry?
   _____
   _____

2. Do you think that Alonso, Antonio, and Sebastian feel guilty about what they did?
   _____
   _____

3. Compare Alonso's reaction to the fiery spirit to Antonio and Sebastian's reaction.

Alonso's reaction	Antonio and Sebastian's reaction

Name: _____

While You Read

Worksheet 13 – Act IV, Scene 1

CD 1
Track 9

A. Read and listen to Act IV, Scene I, pp. 95–108. Prospero has spirits perform for Miranda and Ferdinand. The spirits play the roles of Roman goddesses. In the chart below, describe the gods and goddesses that they mention in the performance.

Name	God or Goddess of . . .
Ceres	
Juno	
Iris	
Venus and Cupid	
Pluto	

B. Answer these questions.

1. Prospero becomes serious after the performance he puts on for Ferdinand and Miranda. What does he say about life and the nature of the world we live in?

   _____

   _____

2. Why do you think Prospero becomes so serious?

   _____

   _____

   _____

C. Circle the correct answer.

1. What do Stephano, Trinculo, and Caliban go through while they follow Ariel's music?
   a. a desert and a river   **b.** mountains and caves   **c.** a swamp, bushes, and thorns

2. Prospero tells Ariel to bring out some _____ in order to attract and trap Stephano, Trinculo, and Caliban.
   a. fine clothes   **b.** gold and jewels   **c.** food and wine

3. Stephano and Trinculo are upset because they lost the _____.
   a. clothes   **b.** wine bottle   **c.** opportunity to kill Prospero

4. _____ is afraid that Prospero will wake up and use his magic on them.
   a. Stephano   **b.** Trinculo   **c.** Caliban

5. Prospero sends _____ running after Stephano, Trinculo, and Caliban.
   a. goblins   **b.** dogs   **c.** Ariel

D. Match each definition to the correct word.

1. _____ regret   **a.** a situation in which events are controlled by magic
2. _____ spell   **b.** a sharp point on a plant or tree
3. _____ thorn   **c.** when you wish you had not done something
4. _____ goblin   **d.** take a person away illegally and by force
5. _____ kidnap   **e.** in the end, after a lot of delays
6. _____ eventually   **f.** an ugly creature, sometimes evil

Name: _____

CD 1
Track 10

A. Read Act V, Scene I, pp. 109–129, and listen to the audio. Then decide if the statements below are true or false. Circle your answers.

1. Ariel convinces Prospero to free Alonso and his men from the trees.	True	False
2. Prospero wanted to kill the men, but now he will free them.	True	False
3. Prospero is going to give up magic after one last spell.	True	False
4. Prospero is angry at Gonzalo for following Alonso.	True	False
5. Alonso apologizes to Prospero and to Miranda.	True	False
6. Antonio apologizes to Prospero.	True	False
7. Prospero forgives Antonio.	True	False
8. Sebastian calls Prospero a good man.	True	False
9. Alonso thinks Miranda is a mortal when he sees her.	True	False
10. The group will sail back to Naples immediately.	True	False

B. Answer the questions.

1. How does Prospero reward Alonso for making him duke again?

_____
_____
_____
_____

2. What is Miranda's reaction when she comes into the room and sees everybody? Explain her reaction.

_____
_____
_____
_____

3. What is Antonio and Sebastian's reaction when they see Stephano, Trinculo, and Caliban arrive? Why is this especially funny?

_____
_____
_____
_____

4. How does Prospero punish Stephano, Trinculo, and Caliban?

_____
_____
_____
_____

5. How does Prospero reward Ariel?

_____
_____
_____
_____

Name: _____

While You Read

Worksheet 15 – Epilogue

CD 1
Track 11

A. Read and listen to the Epilogue on pp. 130–132. Answer the questions.

    1. Who is Prospero talking to? _____

    2. What does Prospero need to get off the island? _____

    3. What expertise has he lost? _____

B. Many believe that Prospero's final speech was also Shakespeare's final speech. What similarities can you find between Prospero and Shakespeare?

Action	Prospero	Shakespeare
Watching action from offstage	When Miranda and Ferdinand declare their love (Act III, Scene I)	As a playwright and actor, Shakespeare probably watched his plays during rehearsals and performances to make sure everything was the way he wanted it to be.
Manipulating other characters, setting them up for "scenes"		
Staging plays		
Inventing strange worlds		
Giving up his "craft"		

Name: _____

Worksheet 16 – Matching Quotes

A. Cut out all the cards and match the quote to the character that said it.

"I don't even know what people outside of this island look like."	**Ariel**
"These strange natives seem so kind. They seem kinder than humans."	**Caliban**
"This monster is in pain. I'll give it some medicine. Maybe I can tame it."	**Fiery Spirit**
"There is only one way you can escape a slow death here on this island. You must be sincerely sorry for what you have done and promise to live good lives from now on."	**Prospero**
"Remember our plan... Let's do it tonight. It'll be easy. They're all exhausted from traveling."	**Antonio**
"Ceres and Iris, come with me, to wish these two prosperity."	**Alonso**

After You Read
Worksheet 16 – Matching Quotes (continued)

"Now my magic is gone from me, only you can set me free."	**Ferdinand**
"If you are real, I give you back your title of duke and ask you to forgive me for the bad things I have done."	**Miranda**
"I'm the only one I care about on this ship! Work, men!"	**Gonzalo**
"I've done good work for you. You made me a promise."	**Stephano**
"He used magic to trick me out of this island. You're brave enough to take revenge."	**Boatswain**
"This must be the goddess that the music was playing for. Are you a goddess or a maiden?"	**Juno**

Important Events in Shakespeare's Life

Approximate Date	What Happened?
1564	William Shakespeare was born in Stratford-upon-Avon on April 23.
1572	Shakespeare (possibly) attended the New King's School in Stratford.
1582	Shakespeare married Anne Hathaway. By 1585, they had three children. We don't know much about his early working life. Some people think that he traveled abroad, that he was a teacher, or that he ran away from Stratford because he was in trouble for stealing a deer.
1587	Shakespeare moved to London. He may have been one of the Queen's Men, which was a group of actors. In 1592, the playwright Robert Greene called Shakespeare an "upstart crow." Greene was jealous of the brilliant new writer.
1593	Shakespeare's friend and fellow playwright, Christopher Marlowe, was killed in a tavern. Around this time, all theaters were shut down because of the plague. When the theaters reopened, Shakespeare joined a company of actors called the Lord Chamberlain's Men.
1597	Shakespeare bought a house in Stratford.
1599	After he finished writing *Henry V*, Shakespeare's company built the Globe, the theater where many of Shakespeare's greatest plays were performed.
1603	Queen Elizabeth I died. James VI became James I, King of England and Wales. King James I became the patron of Shakespeare's theater company, the King's Men. This means that the king supported Shakespeare's company financially.
1613	The Globe burned down. It was rebuilt in 1614.
1614	Shakespeare retired to Stratford and did some writing with John Fletcher, his successor in the King's Men.
1616	Shakespeare died.
1623	Shakespeare's plays were collected by his colleagues John Heminges and Henry Condell and published in a book known as the **First Folio**.

APPENDIX

Shakespeare's Works and Approximate Dates

1590

The Two Gentlemen of Verona

Titus Andronicus

Henry VI, Part 2

Henry VI, Part 3

The Taming of the Shrew

1592

Henry VI, Part 1

Richard III

1593

Venus and Adonis

1594

The Comedy of Errors

Love's Labour's Lost

Romeo and Juliet

The Rape of Lucrece

1595

A Midsummer Night's Dream

King John

Richard II

1596

Henry IV, Part 1

1597

The Merry Wives of Windsor

Henry IV, Part 2

The Merchant of Venice

1598

Much Ado About Nothing

1599

Henry V

Julius Caesar

As You Like It

1600

Hamlet

Twelfth Night

1601

Othello

The Phoenix and the Turtle

Troilus and Cressida

1603

All's Well That Ends Well

1604

Measure for Measure

Timon of Athens

1605

King Lear

1606

Anthony and Cleopatra

Macbeth

1607

Pericles

1608

Coriolanus

1609

A Lover's Complaint

Cymbeline

The Sonnets

1610

A Winter's Tale

1611

The Tempest

1612

IIenry VIII

1613

The Two Noble Kinsmen

Extra Resources

William Shakespeare

- http://folger.edu
- http://shakespeare.palomar.edu
- http://online-literature.com/shakespeare

The Tempest:

- http://www.shakespeare-navigators.com/tempest/index.html
- http://nfs.sparknotes.com/tempest/
- http://absoluteshakespeare.com/guides/tempest/tempest.htm
- http://www.twelfth-night.info/clicknotes/tempest/index.html
- http://www.enotes.com/tempest/
- http://notearama.blogspot.com/2009/12/reading-of-shakespeares-tempest-scene-1.html

Name: _____

A. Your class will now put characters from *The Tempest* on trial for their crimes. Choose from the following ideas, or add some of your own:

- Put Sebastian and Antonio on trial for their crimes and attempted crimes.
- Put Prospero on trial for stealing the island from Caliban and for forcing Caliban and Ariel to be servants.
- Put Caliban, Stephano, and Trinculo on trial for theft and attempted murder.
- *Your idea (optional):* _____

B. To conduct a trial, you will need people to fill several different roles. Decide who will fill each of the following roles in your classroom courtroom:

- The judge: _____
- The jury (4–6 students): _____
- The accused: _____
- The prosecuting attorney: _____
- The defense attorney: _____
- Witnesses: _____

C. Whatever your role is, you will need to think about the case. In the space below, write notes. If you are a lawyer, a witness, or one of the accused, plan what you will say: What are your arguments? What is your evidence? How will you convince the judge and the jury to decide in your favor?

If you are a judge or part of the jury, take notes during the case about the arguments on each side. Try to be fair.

You're ready to start the trial!

_____
_____
_____
_____
_____
_____
_____

Name: _____

Imagine you have just watched a movie adaptation of *The Tempest: The Graphic Novel* on DVD. Now, you click on the "Special Features" in the DVD menu to see the deleted scenes. These are scenes that the director originally wanted to include but had to cut because the movie was too long.

A. Brainstorm ideas for a deleted scene. Choose the best one. In the chart below, make notes about the characters in the scene.

Character	Actor	Clothing	Personality/Emotions

B. Now, write your scene in the form of a screenplay. Include the setting, the dialogue, and the actions of the characters. Here is an example.

```
EXT. Inside Prospero's home, library, day.
ANTONIO enters the library quietly and finds PROSPERO hunched over a
book, reading.
                        PROSPERO
                       (startled)
              Antonio! I did not see you there!
Prospero puts his book down and looks at Antonio.
              What did you come to talk to me about?
                        ANTONIO
                       (angrily)
      What do you mean, what did I come to talk to you about? Have you
                 forgotten that you are the duke?
                        PROSPERO
                       (sternly)
          How can I forget when you won't leave me in peace?
Prospero picks up his book again.
                        ANTONIO
                     (to himself)
      Well, you won't be duke for long . . . I have a way to make you
                        disappear.
```

C. Now, prepare to perform your scene in front of the class. When playing your part, remember your character's personality and the mood of the scene.